BIG BIRD'S BOOK

ABOUT THE *Earth* AND *Sky*

by RAE PAIGE

illustrated by TOM COOKE

Featuring Jim Henson's Sesame Street Muppets

A SESAME STREET / GOLDEN PRESS BOOK
Published by Western Publishing Company, Inc.
in conjunction with Children's Television Workshop.

Consultant

Dr. William A. Gutsch, Jr.
Chairman, American Museum—Hayden Planetarium

Table of Contents

What Is the Earth?

Hi, there! This is the earth!
Isn't it beautiful?

What is the earth?
The earth is the planet we live on. It is also called
the world.

Where does the earth get its light?
From the sun.

What is the earth made of?
Land and water. There are seven continents and
one huge ocean.

What is the equator?
A make-believe line that goes
around the middle
of the earth like a belt.

Rivers, Lakes, and Ponds

Rivers, lakes, and ponds are the homes of
many kinds of fish, frogs, insects, snakes, ducks,
turtles, and geese. Also, many different plants live
in water.

What is a river?
A large stream of fresh,
not salty, water.

What is a lake?
A large body of water that collects in a low place in the ground.

What is a pond?
A small lake.

11

Mountains

Hello, everybody!
It is I, Grover, on top
of a mountain.

What are mountains?
Very high hills. Some mountains are steep and
rocky. Other mountains are round and covered
with trees. Mountain goats, eagles, snow leopards,
elks, and other animals live on the mountains.

**What is the highest mountain
in the world?**
Mount Everest, in Nepal.

What is a volcano?
A mountain that gushes rock
so hot that it runs
like a river.

Caves

What are caves?
Hollow spaces underneath the ground. Caves are
carved by wind, waves, lava, ice, or dripping
water. Bats live in caves.

Look at this, Ernie.
This is a stalactite.
It grows down
from the top
of the cave.

That's nothing, Bert. Look at this!
This is a stalagmite.
It grows up from the ground.

Carlsbad
Caverns

13

Deserts

What is a desert?

A very, very dry place. Rattlesnakes, lizards, rabbits, coyotes, and other animals live in the desert.

What is a cactus?

A desert plant that grows in sand and can live with very little water. Cactus plants have thorns instead of leaves. A cactus stores all its water in its body. Some cacti can go a year without water.

I love the desert. There are sooo many grains of sand to count....One billion one tiny grains of sand, one billion two tiny grains of sand....

What is sand?

Itsy-bitsy, teeny-tiny pieces of rock.

Swamps

What is a swamp?

Soggy, wet land. Flamingos, water moccasins, alligators, snapping turtles, and other animals live in swamps.

I love swamps. Everything's so wet and slimy and yucchy. Speaking of Slimey, he loves it too!

What is the largest swamp in the world?

The Everglades in Florida.

15

Jungles

What is a jungle?

A warm, wet forest with many large trees. Elephants, monkeys, parrots, pythons, and other animals live in the jungle. There are more kinds of trees in the jungle than anywhere else on earth.

There are more insects in the jungle than anywhere else, too.

16

Icebergs

What is an iceberg?

A huge chunk of ice floating in the ocean. Most of an iceberg is underwater. Only the tip of it shows.

Seals like to rest on icebergs. Yah!

How Do People Live Around the World?

Most people live in places where it's cold in the winter and warm in the summer. They wear lots of clothes in the winter and few clothes in the summer.

People who live in cold parts of the world like Alaska have to dress to keep warm.

People who live in warm parts of the world like Hawaii dress to stay cool.

People who live in the Sahara Desert wear long robes and head coverings to protect themselves from the wind and heat.

Trees

Greetings! If you count the rings in a tree trunk you can tell the age of the tree. There's one ring for each year. Let's count. One ring, two rings, three rings, four... This tree is four rings, I mean four years, old!

leaves

branches

trunk

Leaves come in all different shapes and sizes, just as trees do.

palm

This is my leaf collection. Can you make one, too? How many different kinds of leaves can you find where you live?

roots

maple

gingko

oak

mimosa

20

Flowers

My mommy will love these beautiful
and adorable flowers.

How does your garden grow?
The soil of the earth, heat from the sun, and rain
from the sky make plants and flowers grow.

rose

There are many, many different kinds of flowers.
They grow almost everywhere on earth. Some
flowers have a sweet smell.

daisy

carnation

lily

pansy

21

Does Pizza Grow on Trees?

Oh, I am so excited!
I love yummy fresh vegetables!

Where does cheese come from?
Cheese is made from milk.

tomato

pepper

onion

22

Where does flour come from?

Some flour comes from wheat. The wheat is ground up in a mill which turns it into flour.

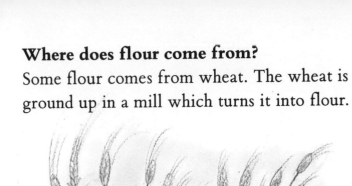

Where do tomatoes and peppers come from?

Plants that grow in the ground.

What about onions?

Onions grow underground in the soil.

Hey, everybody!
With all these delicious things—flour, tomatoes, peppers, onions, and cheese—
I can make PIZZA!

Flour

23

Do Cookies Grow on Trees?

Where does milk come from?
Cows. Mother cows make milk
in their bodies. Farmers milk the cows
and send the milk to a dairy
where it is put into bottles or cartons.

Where does butter come from?
Milk. Grover's great-grandmother used to make
butter in a wooden churn. Now machines do it.

Where does honey come from?
Bees make it from flower nectar, a sweet juice
in flowers. They store it in honeycomb, which is
made out of beeswax.

Where does chocolate come from?
Beans that grow on a tree called the cacao tree.

Where do eggs come from?
Chickens lay eggs.

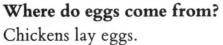

Where does vanilla come from?
Vanilla beans, which grow on a climbing orchid plant.

Hmmm. Milk…butter… honey…chocolate…eggs… vanilla…flour. That's where COOOOKIES come from!

What Makes It Go?

Everything needs fuel for energy.

What makes cars go?
Gasoline.

What makes kids go?
Food.

What makes sailboats go?
Wind.

What makes plants grow?
Sun, soil, and water.

What makes lightbulbs glow?
Electricity.

What makes bicycles go?
Kids.

The Ocean

What is the ocean?
The water that covers most of the earth.

What is a beach?
A sandy place at the edge of the ocean.

Why is the ocean salty?
Rain washes salt from the earth and carries it to the ocean. People shouldn't drink ocean water because the salty water will make them more thirsty.

What makes waves?
Wind blowing across the water makes waves.

Guy Smiley's Wonderful Weather Show

This is Guy Smiley, the world's favorite game show host, welcoming you to the WONDERFUL WEATHER SHOW! Yeah!

The first question is:
What's all around you but can't be seen, tasted, or smelled?
Air! That's right. The air you breathe. Here's a jar of it.

30

The second question is:
What is a cloud?
And the answer is: billions of tiny drops of water and tiny specks of dust that float in the air.

And now,
What is wind?
Right! You're right! Wind is moving air. The only time you can feel air is when it's windy! A storm called a hurricane brings very strong winds.

What is a tornado?
A funnel-shaped cloud with very strong, swirling winds.

The next question is…
What is rain?
Drops of water which fall from the clouds.

What is a flash of light in the sky during a rainstorm?
It's lightning, caused by electricity in the air.

BOOM!

What is the noise you usually hear after a flash of lightning?
How did you know? YES! It's THUNDER!

And now, FOR THE GRAND PRIZE, the last question is...
What is snow?
Water in clouds that freezes and falls to the earth as snowflakes. You did it! You won! So here's your prize from GUY SMILEY'S WONDERFUL WEATHER SHOW...a year's supply, that is 365 days, of... FREE WEATHER!

Did you know that no two snowflakes are exactly alike?

Right. Hold out your mitten and look closely. See? Each snowflake is different.

33

Over the Rainbow

Howdy, pardner! Sometimes when I'm out riding the range I see beautiful rainbows.

What is a rainbow?
A rainbow forms when light shines through
raindrops. A rainbow usually means that a storm is
over, but you might see a rainbow when rain is
falling and the sun is shining at the same time.

What are all the colors in the rainbow?
Red, orange, yellow, green, blue, and violet. Light
is made up of these colors, but you usually can't
see all of them.

The Sun

What is the sun?
A star. It is the closest star to earth.
There could be no life on earth
without the light and heat
from the sun.

What is day?
It is day on the side of the earth that faces the sun.
If the sky isn't cloudy, the people on this side of
the earth can see the sunlight.

Did you know, Tina,
that you should never
look directly at the sun,
even when you're wearing
sunglasses?

That's true, Tessie.
It's very bad
for your eyes.

The Moon

What is the moon?
The large white ball we see in the sky. It is made of moonrocks and soil. It has mountains, valleys, plains, and lots of craters. Since the moon has no air, food, or water, there is no life on the moon.

Where does the moon get its light?
We can see the moon because the sun's light shines on it.

What is night?
It is night on the side of the earth that is facing away from the sun. If the sky isn't cloudy, the people on this side of the earth can see the stars.

Is there a man on the moon, Bert?

Just you and me, Ernie.

Stars

What is a star?
A huge burning ball of fire. Our sun is a star.

What is the Milky Way?
A huge group of stars which is called a galaxy.
Sometimes you can see the Milky Way as a band
of light in the night sky.

The Little Dipper looks like a little spoon. The
star at the end of the Little Dipper's handle is
called the North Star.

The Big Dipper is a group of seven stars which
looks like a ladle or a big spoon.

What is a constellation?
A group of stars that form a pattern or picture.

And what constellation
is that, Tina?

Can't you tell?
That's Cookie Monster.

39

Astro-Bird

Look at me, everybody!
I'm an astro-bird!

What are astronauts?
They are space explorers
who blast off to outer
space in spacecraft.

Why do astronauts wear spacesuits?
Because they have to take their own air with
them. Spacesuits supply the astronauts with air,
and, like big snowsuits, also keep them warm.

Blast-off

Ten, nine, eight, seven, six,
five, four, three, two,
one...BLAST OFF!

Astronauts do not weigh anything
when they are in space. If they don't
wear their seat belts they float around
in the spacecraft.

Spacecraft

What is LEM?
The Lunar Excursion Module (LEM) is the name
of the spacecraft that actually landed on the moon.

What is a space station?
Space stations are laboratories that can be sent
into space.

What is the Space Shuttle?

The Space Shuttle is a spacecraft that takes off like a rocket and lands back on earth like an airplane. It can be flown over and over again. It can be used to put satellites into space and to fix broken ones.

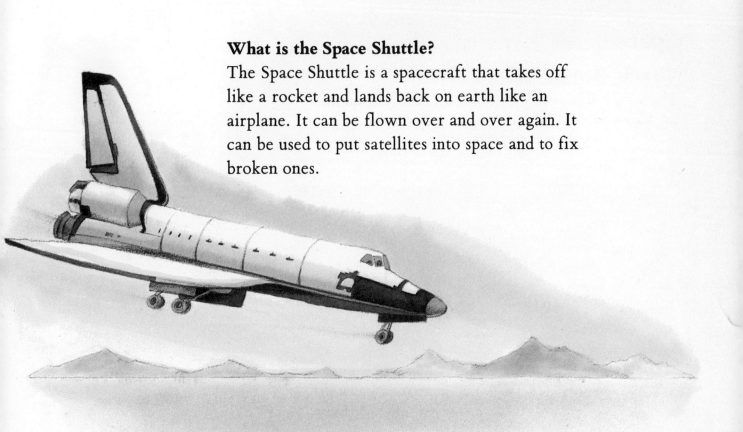

What is a satellite?

A satellite is a machine that is launched into space by a rocket or the Space Shuttle. Different satellites do different kinds of work. Some send television pictures from one part of the world to another.

43

The Solar System

What is the solar system?
The sun and the nine planets that travel around the sun.

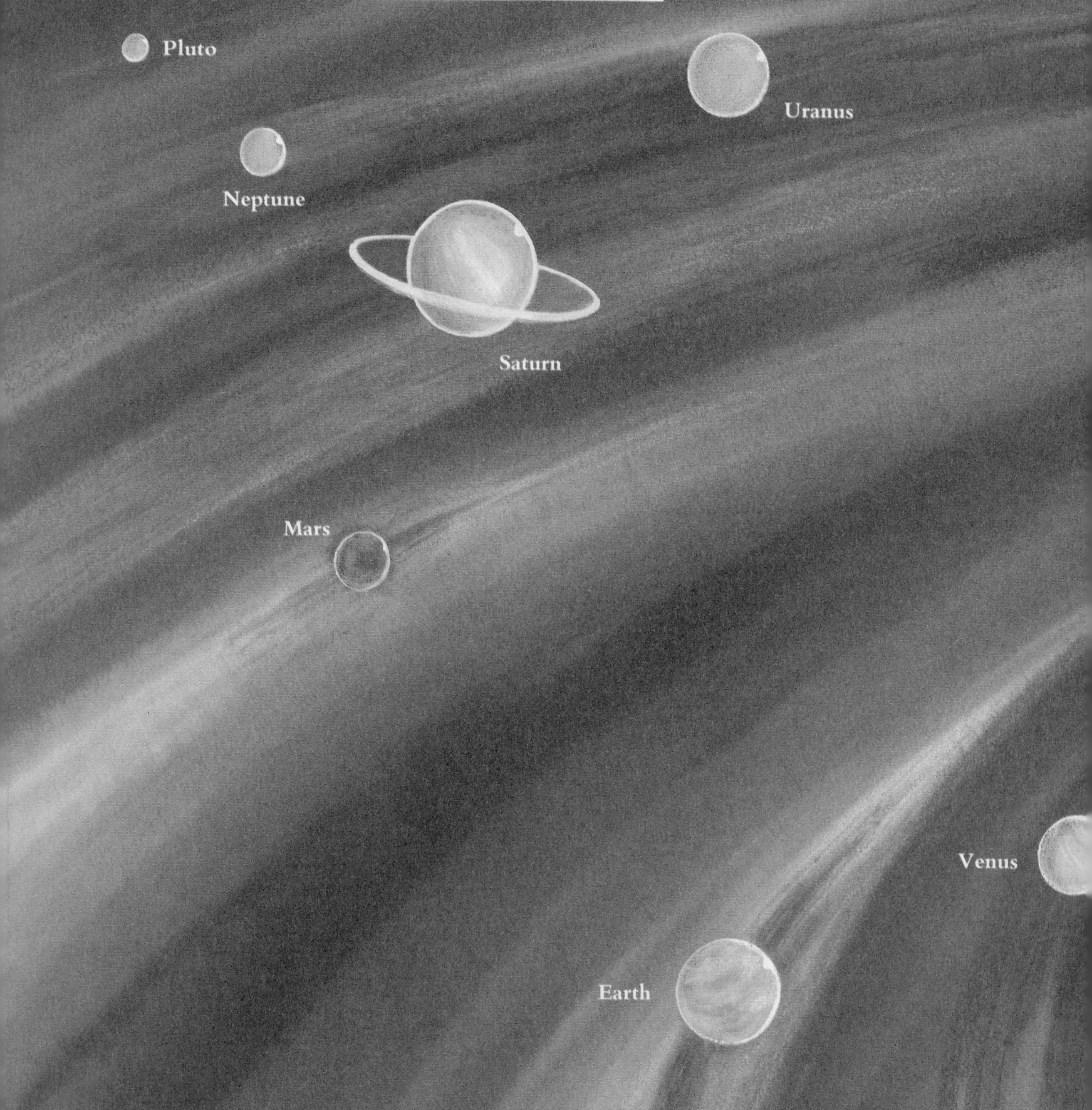

Pluto

Uranus

Neptune

Saturn

Mars

Venus

Earth

Jupiter

Mercury

What is the largest planet?
Jupiter.

What is the smallest planet?
Pluto.

Which planet can come closest to the earth?
Venus.